This book belongs to:

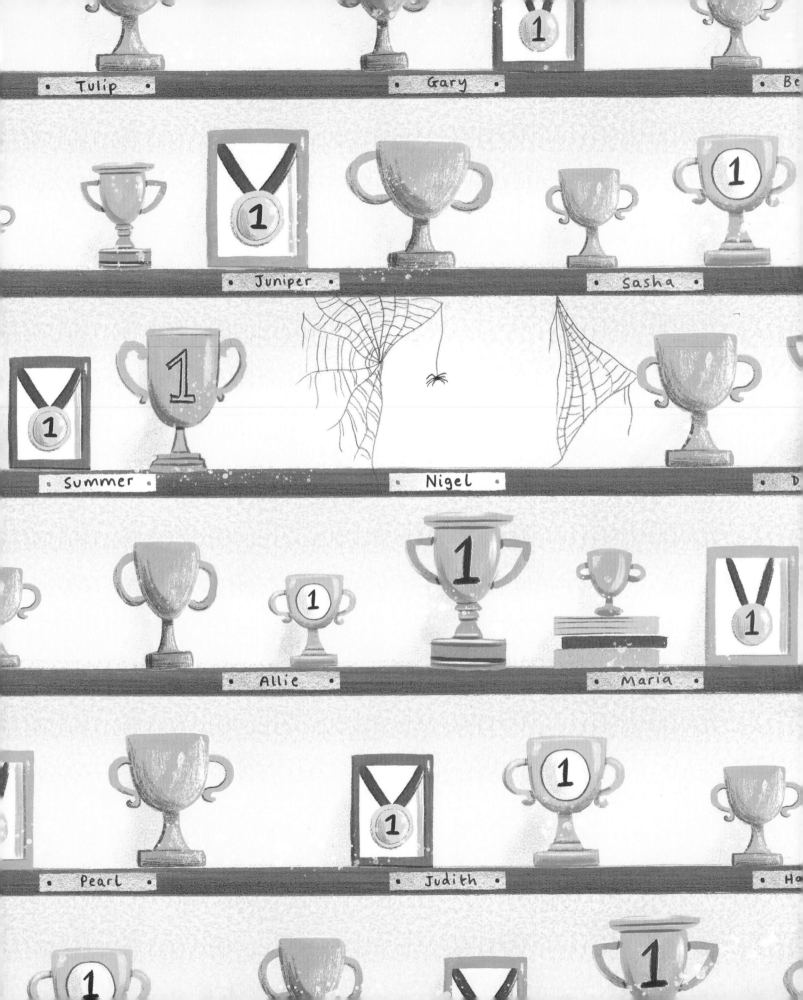

For Scarlett and Tabitha

A TEMPLAR BOOK

First published in the UK in 2020 by Templar Books,
an imprint of Bonnier Books UK,
The Plaza, 535 King's Road, London, SW10 0SZ
www.templarco.co.uk
www.bonnierbooks.co.uk

ISBN 978-1-78741-661-1 (paperback)
ISBN 978-1-78741-791-5 (eBook)

This book was typeset in Trocchi
The illustrations were created with gouache paint,
coloured pencils and digital painting

Edited by Katie Haworth
Designed by Olivia Cook
Production by Emma Kidd

Printed in China

FSC
www.fsc.org

MIX
Paper from
responsible sources
FSC® C104723

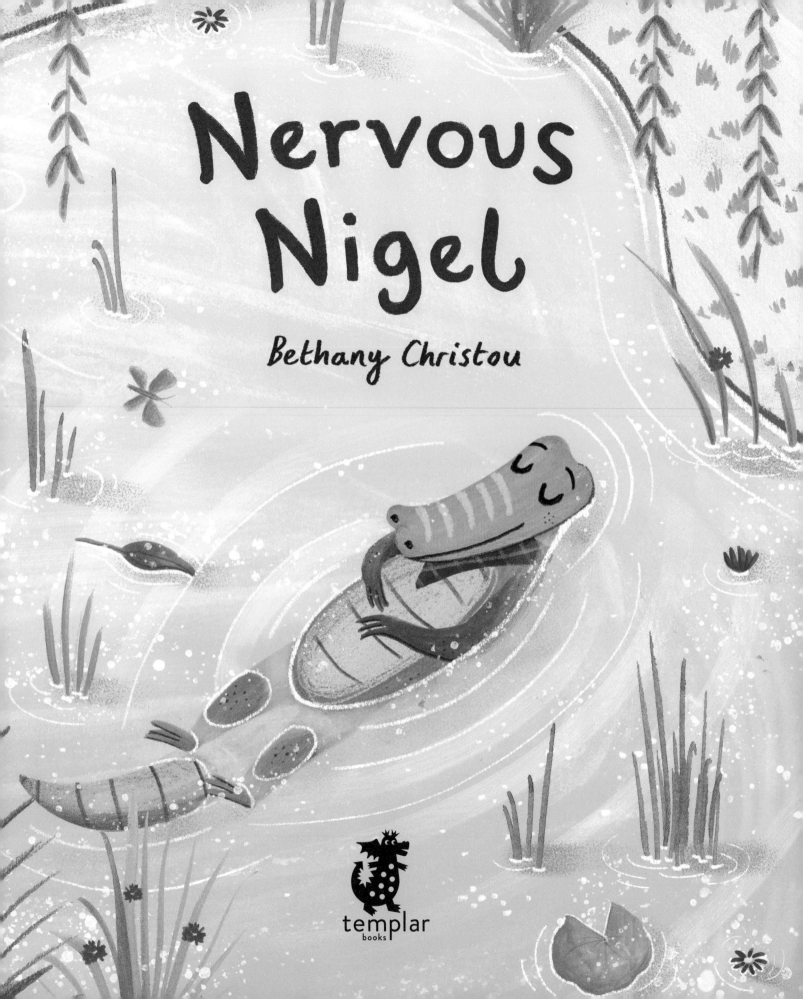

Nervous
Nigel

Bethany Christou

templar
books

Nigel came from
a long line of
greats.

Every crocodile in his family was a **champion**.

Nigel's mum was the fastest
swimmer in crocodile history.

JUNIPER
RECORD BREAKER, REPTILE WORLD CHAMPIONSHIP

GRANNY LOU
GOLD MEDAL, BACKSTROKE, CROC GAMES

His sister, Summer, could win
marathons with her eyes shut.

SUMMER
FIRST PLACE, RIVER NILE HALF MARATHON

Nigel's other sister, Bonnie, was the first crocodile to get a perfect diving score . . .

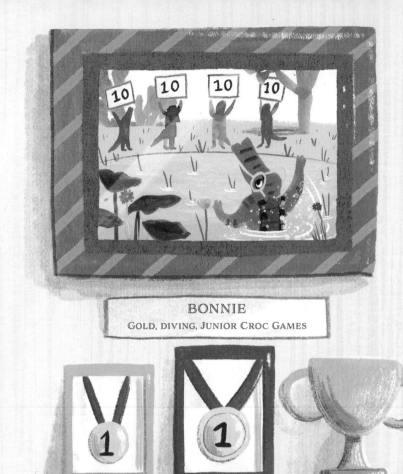

BONNIE
GOLD, DIVING, JUNIOR CROC GAMES

. . . and his brother, Ralf, was captain of the water polo team.

RALF
SNAP SCHOOL WATER POLO TEAM

Nigel's family wanted him to be a champion swimmer.
And Nigel *did* love swimming.

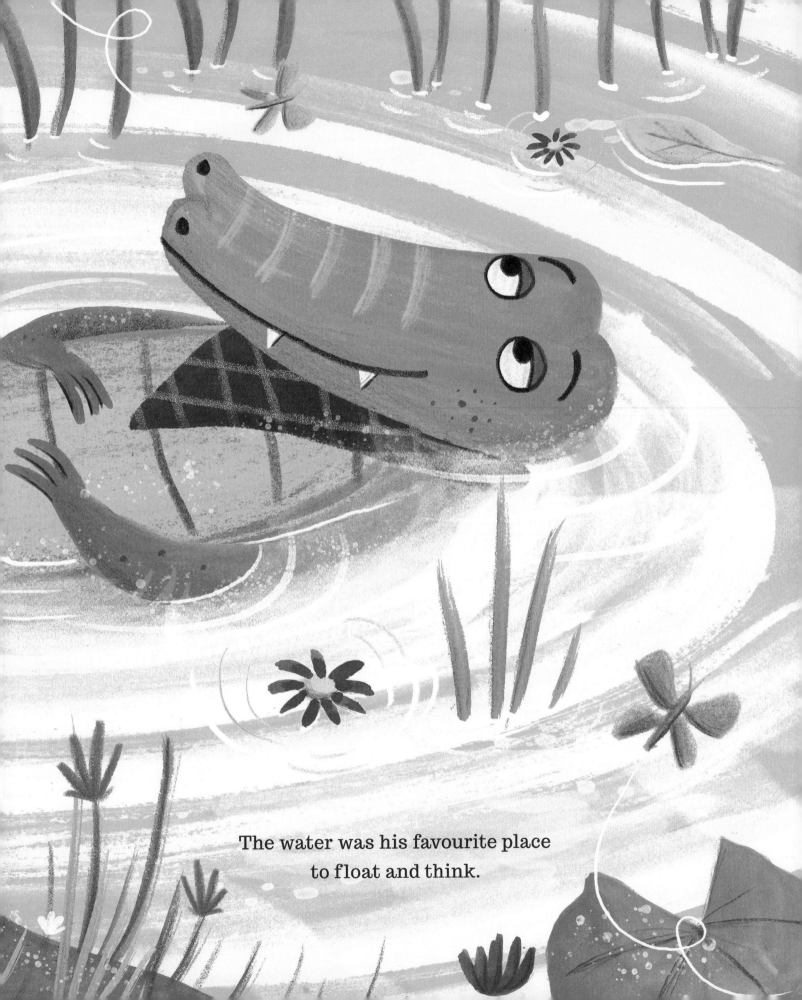

The water was his favourite place
to float and think.

But as soon as Nigel started training,
being in the water didn't seem fun any more . . .

Once the whistle blew,
his heart started **thumping**.

GO! GO! GO!

When the shouting got louder,
his teeth started **chattering**.

FASTER!

As his mum shouted,
his tail started *trembling*.

But he couldn't tell
his mum how he felt,
so he always said . . .

That was a
lovely swim!

Then, one day, his family told him
they'd entered him in his first competition.

Nigel began to **panic**.

His heart started **thumping**.
His tail started *trembling*.
His teeth started chattering.

But he couldn't let his family know,
so all he said was . . .

That night, Nigel couldn't sleep. His head was full of all the **terrible things** that could happen.

Nigel decided that he had to get out of the competition.

But no matter what he tried . . .

. . . and he tried a LOT of things . . .

. . . nothing seemed to work.

There was only one thing left to do,
and that was tell the **truth**.

Nigel had to let his family know how he felt.

Heart **thumping**, tail *trembling*,
teeth **chattering**, Nigel approached
the kitchen door.

He asked, "What would you think if a crocodile **didn't** want to be a champion?"

His family were bewildered.

Nigel's mum and brother and sisters did
their best to reassure him.

But **nothing** made him feel better,
and soon Nigel wished he hadn't said anything at all.

The day of the competition arrived.

And even though he tried to hide it . . .

. . . Nigel was **shaking** with nervousness.

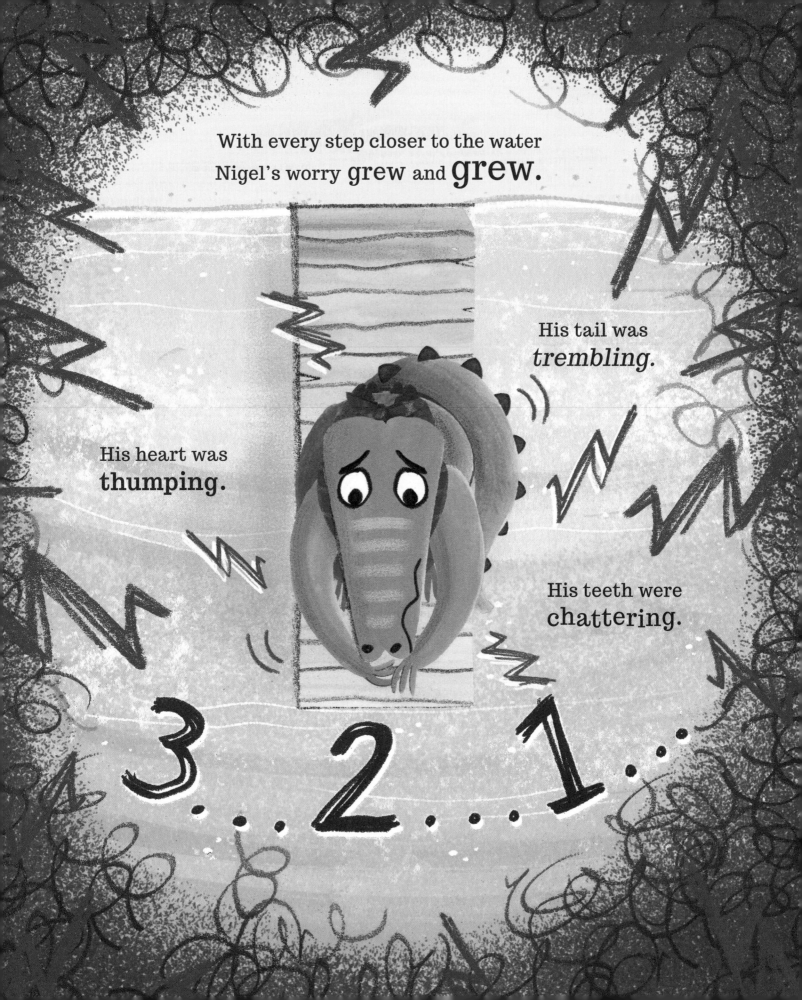

Finally, Nigel couldn't hide it any longer.
He was **too nervous** to race.

Nigel's family rushed over to him.
Nigel was **certain** that he'd disappointed them . . .

. . . and he ran off before
they could finish speaking.

Further down the river, Nigel did
his best to forget what had happened.
Floating usually helped him feel calm,
but today he just felt lost.

Then, he heard
a little voice . . .

Excuse me?

It was a frog. She asked Nigel to give her a ride across the water.

Nigel was only too pleased to help.

The frog thought Nigel looked sad, so she
asked him what the problem was. Nigel told her.

But the frog didn't agree.

And that gave Nigel a brilliant idea . . .

Nigel's
FLOATING TRANSPORT
and
SCENIC TOURS

Nigel's Floating Transport
and Scenic Tours was
a **great** success.

Nigel didn't need to rush or race and he didn't have to worry or lose sleep.

Now he could float and think all he liked.

BOOK HERE

And it seemed that lots of other animals liked to do the same.

Nigel wasn't winning any medals,
but he was doing something he loved.

We're sorry we didn't listen to you, Nigel.

We just want you to be happy!

And for him,
that was enough.

Also available:

ISBN: 978-1-78370-870-3 (paperback)
ISBN: 978-1-78741-602-4 (eBook)